Praise for *Miss*

MISSING SIGNAL
SEB DOUBINSKY

Meerkat Press
Atlanta

ISBN-13 - 978-1-946154-11-8 (Paperback)
ISBN-13 - 978-1-946154-12-5 (eBook)

Library of Congress Control Number: 2018947598

Printed in the United States of America

Published in the United States of America by
Meerkat Press, LLC, Atlanta, Georgia
www.meerkatpress.com

To Acep Hale

"L'histoire n'existe pas"

—William Burroughs, *The Western Lands*

"Someone's been killed. I want you to see the corpse."

—Michelangelo Antonioni, *Blow-Up*

I

a man claiming to be

I

"A man claiming to be an ex-member of the ultra-secret Alien Containment Force, known as ACF or Force 136, has agreed to meet us in a secret place and tell us what is really going on behind the official UFO scene. Here is what he told us and it is terrifying."

Terrence's eyes moved away from the PC screen as he reached out for a cigarette. The man talking had a bad '70s haircut and a drooping mustache. The other man sitting in front of him, half-hidden in the shadow, wore a pair of jeans and a loose red polo shirt. He had no watch. There were two cameras, alternating on the faces—one pimply, nervous and awed, the other dark, invisible and mysterious.

They even had the voice modified, for security reasons, but Terrence knew what it sounded like. He also knew that "the man claiming to be" wore a wig, colored contact lenses and a set of false teeth masking the real ones. The missing watch was an important detail: it made identification more difficult. A watch is a signature object. Like shoes. The man had also bought a type of shoes he usually never wore.

Terrence smiled, listening to the mysterious man speak, and looked down at some papers spread before him. He chewed on the tip of a pencil that served as a poor substitute for a cigarette and nodded to himself. All the necessary information—or rather disinformation—had been passed. Another worldwide alien conspiracy theory confirmed. The New Petersburg Counter-Intel Department had done an amazing piece of work.

Terrence patted himself on the back. *Good job, officer.* It had been a tough mission: he had really sweated like a pig underneath that horrible wig, and the new shoes had maimed his toes.

2

The Counter-Intel Department cafeteria was known to be one of the best in the New Petersburg Armed Forces, so Terrence chose the strange-looking pastry without any fear and put it on his tray, next to the Styrofoam coffee cup. Whatever it was, it would taste good—or at least, better than in all the other armed forces cafeterias.

He added milk to his coffee and went to sit at a free table in the large and almost empty space. He felt like a cigarette, but there was a complete smoking ban, even in the immediate vicinity of the building. He took out a nicotine gum and stuck it in his mouth. The foul spearmint taste ruined both his craving and the taste of his coffee.

The elevator was empty and he smiled at his reflection in the mirror. He sometimes wondered why they put mirrors in elevators. Were there hidden cameras behind, filming them? There were cameras everywhere, after all—why not here? The idea made him smile. It looked crooked in the mirror.

ㄩ

Was his life a series of paragraphs or a long seamless succession of events? Was his "I" a heavy solid object in the center or a split-up entity, shining differently in 10,000 worlds? Was he passing through endless mirrors or was he stuck on a single reality plane? Was he an endless illusion or a limited materiality? Was he? Simply that: was he?

5

Terrence sat down at his desk, putting his coffee next to the computer keyboard. He looked at the screen and his mind drifted to chapter four. If Terrence ever had to choose a chapter number for his life right now, it would have been four. Not quite the beginning. Not even the beginning of the beginning: the possibility of something happening in the next chapters, long before the end. But he was 39 now, and he felt he was way beyond chapter four. Probably more like eleven or twelve. So four was wishful thinking. And it might become nostalgia soon. Sighing, he returned to his notes. Sometimes he let his mind drift too much.

6

Terrence's office was small, located at the end of the corridor in the C.I.D. building, which was situated on the Pappy Boyington Air Force Base on the outskirts of New Petersburg. It was kind of gloomy, with a single chair, a small metal desk for his laptop, no window and a single bookshelf. Perfect for the job, actually. The walls were painted a dull pigeon gray, and the only splash of color was a poster of Antonioni's *Blow-Up*. He had seen the movie once on his computer and had loved it, because of its beautiful emptiness, which he felt mirrored his own. Terrence seldom worked there, as he was in the field a lot, on special assignments. He even missed it, sometimes.

7

The notes consisted mostly of a list of websites. A long one. Some were crossed out. Inactive or deactivated. The latter thanks to Terrence, generally. He often thought of himself as a "trickster," these old gods or half-gods that could never be fully trusted or relied on—Loki and Coyote were the most famous, but there were many, many of them. Always changing face, always offering poisoned help. His personal email was ulysses@np.net. The greatest trickster of them all. And he was a man. A human being, working for his beloved City-State, like Terrence did. Exactly like Terrence did. Sometimes he imagined being interviewed for a magazine.

Q: Is it difficult to work as a trickster? I mean, nobody really likes you, nobody trusts you; you have no real friends . . .

A: No, it's not difficult at all. It's fun. A lot of fun. I like to have fun alone. It's the best. Look at me: I'm laughing. I'm alone, and I'm laughing.

8

Sometimes things have to remain secret. You are very young, but you understand that. You are eleven years old, but you get it. Don't tell anyone. Ever. Because, if you do, nobody is going to look at you the same way. And your life will be ruined forever, and it won't even be your fault.

9

When not in the field, Terrence spent most of his days on the computer. He surfed old sites, checked out new sites, answered emails, wrote emails, deleted emails, chatted under various aliases, accepted appointments, canceled appointments, ordered food, watched movies. He actually had a list of his aliases and access codes, because he had so many of them. Fifty-seven, to be precise. He had counted. Sometimes it was hard for him to recall his real name. Terrence Kovacs. It sounded weird to his own ears when he said it out loud. Alien. Yeah, alien. The word made him smile.

10

He checked the inner pocket of his jacket before locking the door of his office. The plane ticket was there. New Belleville, flight AP 202, 10:45 a.m. He was going to attend the International Unidentified Flying Phenomenons Specialists' Conference, which opened this weekend. He would appear as the world-famous John Tammen, founder of the world-respected International UFO Reference Site. Another long makeup session—he actually had to dye his hair a strange silvery white, like the Moon King. He would look spectacular.

II

As usual, he walked to the subway station, which wasn't very far. No car for him. It was too easy to trace and he didn't like to drive. Like many people, he was scared of dying in a freak accident. His absent-mindedness could be dangerous. The late spring evening was warm, and the sky had this blue melancholic hue that reminded him that he had a heart. Somewhere in there.

12

The apartment was empty, as usual, and filled with golden light. Perfect balance. He realized he was hungry. As usual, balance never lasted long.

Later, when he went to bed, he wondered where light went when darkness came. Was it absorbed by darkness? Did it become a part of darkness, or did it hide somewhere invisible until it could come out again? Of course, the rotation of Earth around the sun explained most of it, that day was simply pushed away by the night. But it didn't cover all of it. Nothing was ever fully explained, like you can know how lightning is created, but you can't explain why poor Michael was hit by it, and not one of the other forty-five kids running in the field, himself included. That would never be explained. Never. And yet it had its importance. Why Michael? Why *him*?

13

Fate and chances had always fascinated Terrence since he was a child. Maybe fate and chances were the same thing, under a different name. Or God, even. If He or She or It existed, which Terrence doubted. His radical skepticism had been one of the major reasons he had joined the C.I.D. and he had scored a hundred percent on hoaxes and urban legends. The other reason was that he was colorblind and he couldn't become a pilot in the Air Force.

14

That night Terrence dreamt he was making love to a beautiful girl from the 1960s. It was his room, but they definitely were in the '60s. The girl kept smiling while they did their thing. She also smiled afterwards, and even laughed. Terrence felt terrific.

15

It was a strange feeling to be going to the airport on Thursday. It felt like he was ahead on the weekend. It wasn't unpleasant, but Terrence felt somewhat awkward, like he was cheating, and he was a deeply honest man, which made his job a paradox: you had to be dedicated to the truth in order to be lying all the time. He looked out the cab window. Everybody else was on their way to work. He almost envied them.

16

Terrence stopped by the duty free perfume and cosmetics shop to smell some of the latest men's fragrances. He had always had a keen smelling sense and perfume was one of his secret passions. He could tell almost any cologne that a person was wearing, and when he couldn't, he had to stop that very person and ask her or him. He had a perfume atlas in his head, categorized by colors and warmth. The one he was smelling right now, *Ouija*, by Poe & Friends, was dark blue and cold. He actually liked it. Quite a lot. It reminded him of his soul, if he had one. It would smell exactly like this. When he stood in front of the cash register, he suddenly felt strange buying his own soul.

17

He washed his hands for a long time in the bathroom, not because they were especially dirty, but because he was looking at the man in the mirror, with the silvery white hair, the blue eyes and the horn-rimmed glasses.

18

To Terrence, airports were the micro-utopias of capitalism: everybody was under constant surveillance, the prices were the same in all the shops and the cleaning personnel were underpaid immigrants. Plus you had the V.I.P. lounges and special shortcuts for the very rich. The perfect world.

Of course, Terrence was no Communist, nor had he any revolutionary streak in him. But he had a critical mind, which was how he got that job in the first place, and he couldn't help reflecting about the environment he was in. He was analytical and rational. That's how he managed to keep so many identities—each had a purpose, a delimitation and a common objective: to protect New Petersburg's security and identify possible threats.

This time, he would be John Tammen in New Belleville, the famous UFOlogist and conspiracy theorist. He had brought a recent and thick UFO "true story" bestseller to read on the plane, to appear more credible. It asserted that the Apollo missions were all faked in order to protect the secret Nazi planetary government that was hiding underneath the moon's surface and that furnished the Western Alliance with new weapon blueprints. It would be hard for Terrence not to laugh out loud, but his psychological training had been perfect. He only laughed when he wanted to. Even when alone at home. Which he always was.

19

The airport in New Belleville looked exactly like the one in New Petersburg, with the same shops, the same travelers and the same immigrant cleaning personnel. All the shops were the same, selling the same products for the same discount price. Terrence thought it was stupid for airports to have names. "Same Airport, different place" would suffice.

20

Henri Gaillard was waiting for him. He was the New Belleville specialist on all UFO conspiracy matters, and he sounded so convinced by even the craziest theories that Terrence sometimes wondered if he was, like Terrence, an infiltrated special agent. A tall, dry silhouette with a weird mop of reddish hair and thick Stephen King glasses, Henri was perfect for the job—whichever it was. His age was impossible to tell—anywhere from twenty-five to forty-five. Maybe an alien infiltrator?

"Welcome to Belleville, John! So good to see you again!"

Even the exaggerated French accent sounded too perfect, like lifted from an old American musical comedy. *Too much paranoia kills paranoia*, Terrence thought and smiled.

"Happy to be here too."

It wasn't even a lie. He has always dreamed of visiting New Belleville. Deep down inside, he was like everybody else, a bit of a romantic soul.

21

The hotel room was small, but clean. Henri had left him so he could shower and rest. The conference started at 10 a.m. the next morning, at the Grande Salle de la Mutualité. It would last three days, which meant that Terrence would be back in New Petersburg by Tuesday.

He thought about extending his trip a bit—he could always tell the higher-ups that he had someone else to see or some info he had to verify. This job left him basically free and everything was paid for. Ideal position. Except you had to lie all the time and had no close friends.

But that was more Terrence's own choice: he knew a couple of guys who worked along the same lines who had lots of friends, and some were even married. They just lied to their friends and spouses about their jobs. And that was something Terrence couldn't accept and couldn't do. He had moral limits, even if they seemed sometimes blurred. He remembered the 1960s girl from his dreams. He could never have lied to her. Never.

22

Terrence walked to the restaurant where he was supposed to meet Henri and a few other people he didn't know. He could have taken a taxi, but he wanted to get a feel of the mythical city. So many artists had lived there, so many writers and movie directors! Of course they were all dead now, and New Belleville built on the right bank, with its towering skyscrapers and tacky shopping malls had nothing much to do with the past—but still.

The humans had this incredible power to project themselves into something that once was, and feel part of it—as he did at this very moment. He felt he could actually write a novel. And a good one, at that.

23

Terrence stopped for a second and looked at the river Séquane quietly flowing under the bridge like spilled green broth. He remembered paintings, old black and white photographs, avant-garde films—the river always seemed so beautiful. But in reality . . . He shrugged sadly. It was like waking up in the morning after a night of drunken sex: the disappointment was tremendous.

24

After the dinner, he decided against taking a cab back to his hotel, although they had the reputation for being cheap. New Belleville definitely was a city for walking.

The dinner had been alright—the food was excellent, and so was the wine. *Bien sûr.* And the company had been—interesting. Besides Henri, there had been a New Moscow woman with a bad hairdo and purple nails, a New Babylon retired professor with glasses so thick his eyes looked like tiny blue emojis and a Viborg City young man who sounded so dumb and naive that Terrence still wondered if it had been an act.

The discussion had revolved around the Black Shield, that mysterious object that was supposed to orbit around the Earth. As Terrence Kovacs, Counter-Intel officer, he knew it didn't exist and was only a dead Eastern Confederation satellite wreckage from the '60s, but as John Tammen he engaged the conversation and came up with his favorite theory—the one he was famous for—which was that the Black Shield was an alien spaceship from another dimension, sucked into ours by secret military experiments gone terribly wrong. What he didn't know was if there were still aliens inside, or if they were all dead.

"I think they're still alive" Vera, the Moscow woman had said. "I've got secret contacts who told me so. They even have a recording . . ."

The conversations kept on this track and similar ones until the end of the meal. Terrence shrugged in the mild spring evening. Business as usual. He would have to check these people out on Intel back at the hotel.

25

The woman was legit—a New Moscow physicist who had been publishing a blog on UFOs since she was a student. No connection could be traced to any secret or disinformation service. Her secret contacts must have been phonies.

The New Babylon professor was also in the clear. Terrence actually remembered reading something by him a long time ago—ancient aliens stuff. He might even have used some of his crackpot theories in another conference or interview, a long time ago.

He couldn't find anything about the young man from Viborg City, though, which was strange. Not a single article, blog or even reference. He would have to question Henri about how they had met, etc.

Viborg City was an ally of Petersburg and Babylon, and part of the Western Alliance. But he knew they had been working on some ultra-secret AI stuff recently and might be looking for ways to access information or contacts through unconventional channels.

The irrational was the greatest weakness of any political system; its Achilles' heel. Anybody, smart or stupid, could be attracted by it. Many conspiracy theorists had a completely rational side—quite a few had university degrees and were functioning perfectly well socially.

Some respected scientists also believed in aliens and ghosts. Hell, almost half the world's population worshiped one god or another. That's why things had to be kept under control, because between the lies you could find true info about secret military or scientific projects that one of these otherwise very rational loonies was leaking, without realizing what he or she was doing. Damage control was Terrence's primary mission. The second was how to identify and use the weaknesses of the other sides.

He checked his various email boxes. There was nothing interesting, just the usual bullshit and pseudo-secret crap. Nothing either on his personal address. He had only subscriptions there, as well as a very few selected friends, most of them colleagues.

Jet-lag suddenly hit him, and he shut down his computer before getting between the fresh-smelling sheets of his hotel bed and dreaming about smiling naked '60s beauties.

26

The convention was held in a beautiful building of the Left Bank, all in '30s style. The only problem was it was so overheated that Terrence was afraid his dye and makeup would run. Fortunately, they didn't and his conference went well. He got a standing ovation and had to answer questions for more than an hour.

27

"Loved it! What a great talk!" Henri said afterwards, as they were having a drink at the bar. "You always come up with the best questions and the best explanations."

Terrence smiled and nodded.

Of course, he thought. *Of course. That's my job.*

28

The chance of being hit by lightning is 1 in 960,000. Which means there is always a chance. Always.

29

New Belleville at night, walking alone. Terrence had lied to Henri and told him he had someone to meet for dinner. *An old friend from New Pete. Moved here years ago.* Could have been true too. The advantage of being a fictional character: anything was possible. You just had to rewrite your bio all the time.

New Belleville—the old part, at least—was a maze of transparencies and shadows. He had a feeling anything could happen here, and he remembered walking up the Rue Saint-Jacques—the old Roman Cardo, the north-south street they always traced when building new cities—that it was considered one of the most mysterious and occult places in the world. Not that he believed in any of this, of course, but being hyper-rational didn't mean being insensitive to the po- etics of places and landscapes. As a child, he had loved ghost stories, fantasy and, of course, science fiction.

⅃O

Yes, of course—Science Fiction. You had to, you had no choice. You had to find an explanation. Like you always do. Because otherwise they would lock you up. They would lock you up and you would never come out.

⊒I

Back in his hotel room, Terrence reviewed the intel he had reaped during the day. The most intriguing had been a communication from a woman from New Shanghai, who had "confirmed" allegations of a lot of UFO sightings in the Chinese Southwestern Mountains.

This was interesting because there were rumors about the Chinese Confederation building a huge communication center—some even spoke of a super quantum computer—in the area. He had noted her name down and he would run a quick check back home.

There had been two or three other interesting presentations, but nothing really new. Terrence felt good seeing that his disinformation work still functioned perfectly well. He counted no less than twenty-two references to his interviews under different aliases, and thirty-seven to his various web pages.

Tomorrow, Henri's new friends would make their communications. Terrence would carefully listen to that Viborg City boy, see what he had to say—or what he wanted not to say. Which was always the more interesting.

32

Sometimes everything stopped like a scratched vinyl, the diamond-head hopping off with a screeching white noise. Then someone would lift it and start the record again. Or not. That day, nobody had done it for poor little Michael, hit by lightning.

33

He woke up trying to remember his dream. Then he realized that it might be better if he didn't. Things that weren't meant to be, shouldn't be brought back. So many stories, so many myths.

Learn your lesson, boy. For once.

∃Ч

The second and last day of the conference went pretty much like the first one, which was no surprise, except for the Viborg City young man's communication. He talked about the Black Shield and contradicted "John Tammen's" theory, claiming that it was just a decoy, covering up for a huge alien control system aimed at keeping Earth under its mental control. He said that the Black Shield was just the wreck of a 1960s satellite used by the Aliens as a "thing of interest" for UFO lovers in order to hide a real secret device he dubbed the "Dream Machine," and which was invisible to the human eye and radars.

The fact that he knew the truth about the satellite wreck had surprised Terrence, even more so as it was set in an apparently paranoid rant. He could have laughed at this, like some of the others had impolitely done out loud, but the kid didn't seem crazy. At least, he hadn't seemed crazy when they'd had dinner together with Henri the other night. True, he hadn't talked much, but when he had, he made sense—at least, as much as had Henri and his own character, John Tammen.

Terrence looked for him at the closing reception after the conference, but couldn't find him. He wanted to check if the name he had punched into his intelligence data check system the previous night had been spelled right.

"Thomas Thomasen" or "Thomassen." Maybe he had forgotten a letter. Those Nordic names were something special. He would have loved to be able to double-check the dude's conference badge.

2

element not found

I

"Anything we should worry about?" Colonel Bergman asked him, putting aside the file report on his desk without even glancing at it.

Terrence told him about Thomasen or Thomassen, wondering if Bergman ever read his reports, or if he just passed them on without ever opening the file. The colonel nodded sharply. A thin man with steel-rimmed glasses, Bergman looked the part of a Cold War intelligence officer. Even his uniform seemed outdated.

"You think there is a need for a counter-intel operation?"

Terrence shrugged.

"Not sure yet, sir. I don't know what impact his theory has had. He doesn't have a web site. He isn't listed anywhere. He can't be 'official,' that's for certain. Viborg City would never launch such a hostile operation against us—if it is a hostile operation. His theory attacks all other current decoys."

The colonel rubbed his chin.

"His theory sounds crazier than everything else, sure, but what if people want to believe what he says? Why would that be a problem for us?"

Terrence didn't know if his commanding officer was playing dumb or if he was really that dumb. Actually, he had been wondering about that since Bergman had replaced Strozzi, whom Terrence still missed. A true, hardworking professional, who could anticipate peril in a fraction of a second. He had created "John Tammen," which had been a streak of genius.

"With all due respect, sir, we have managed to control efficiently all Black-Shield theories circulating at the moment, and use them in any way we chose. This has helped us minimize dangerous leaks in our defense program. If a new theory comes out, stating that all other theories are bullshit, we can be in big trouble."

"I see," the colonel said, reclining in his articulated design leather armchair. "I see. What do you suggest, then?"

"Nothing yet. I don't know if any damage has been done, but we should try to gather sources on this Thomassen. Also from legit organizations, sir."

"You mean like Viborg City Intel?"

Terrence nodded.

"That can backfire easily. If Viborg City thinks we're trying to monitor them, they might react badly. Not that we ever had any problems with them, but who knows these days?"

Terrence knew what the colonel was referring to. Viborg City had launched a solo crusade against the Eastern Alliance, trying to blow on the Cold War embers for reasons unknown. The other Western Alliance cities were worried that this could escalate and there were tensions between allies at the moment. Bergman obviously didn't want to make things worse.

"Just an idea," Bergman added, as Terrence began rising from his chair. "Could this be personal?"

Terrence sat back down.

"How do you mean?"

"Well, your theory, through your 'John Tammen' site, is definitely the most popular and accepted in these loony circles. Maybe that Thomassen guy is jealous. Maybe he wants to destroy you. Or maybe someone else does and sent him your way. Might have nothing to do with geopolitics and international tensions—but you. Just you. Think about that. Dismissed."

2

Personal? Really? How could anything be personal against a man with 57 aliases? What could be personal against a man who didn't exist? A man pretending to be all the time and who never really was anytime? Or was he? But who was he?

"My name is Terrence Kovacs," he said, looking at himself in the elevator mirror. The image nodded.

That evening he felt he needed some fun and decided to go drinking. None of his usual drinking buddies, Frank, Todd or Louie, were free, so he decided to go on a binge by himself. Yes, it was the middle of the week. Yes, he would feel miserable the next day. Yes, he felt lonely as hell, but hey, that was life. His life. The only life he *really* knew.

4

He went to George's and had a couple of scotches on the rocks with a little water. He chatted up some blonde, but it turned out she was waiting for her boyfriend. None of the other women in the bar were free, nor his type. He decided the only women he could face tonight were strippers. At least you didn't need to chat them up to get them naked. And your loneliness would remain intact all the way through.

5

The girl moved beautifully under the changing spotlights. Terrence had chosen her because of her afro wig, which made her look like a '70s B-Movie actress. Her black skin reflected the light in incredible nuances, spreading over her sweaty body. Her perfect breasts swayed inches away from his nose. *Look, but don't touch. Look, but don't touch.* He could almost hear his mother's voice when, as a kid, they had walked down the toy store alley in a supermarket.

Later, when he did his thing in the bathroom, remembering her incredible body, he imagined her smiling and he was overwhelmed with pleasure and love.

6

For the next two weeks, Terrence kept an eye open to see if Thomassen or Thomasen had posted his theory anywhere on the Net, or if there were any follow-ups on his New Belleville conference. Strangely, even Henri, who had introduced him, said nothing about it in his blog. Thomassen wasn't even mentioned in his summary of the New Belleville events. Terrence began to wonder if he had hallucinated, pure and simple. Maybe it was best to let it go, he thought. It was nothing. Only a young kid trying to make an impression.

Just to make sure he hadn't gone mad, he sent Henri an email asking him if he had heard anything from Thomassen, because he thought his theory had been "interesting" and wanted to contact him.

In his reply Henri told him that Thomassen (he also wrote it with double "s") had disappeared immediately after his conference and that no one (probably meaning himself only) had heard from him since. He added that this was very mysterious and that he (John Tammen) should contact him if he heard anything, because he would want to hear more about the kid's surprising and mind-boggling theory too.

The plot thickens, Terrence thought, but he was glad to see that he wasn't going insane.

7

On the short clip you can see a forest at twilight. Suddenly two light orbs appear out of nowhere, dancing above the trees. A voice exclaims *Oh look! That's incredible! That's incredible!* The orbs are filmed closer and they seem to be made of metal. The voice continues its exclamations.

Terrence looked at the clip he had put together. It would be going live on one of his 57 sites and would become viral almost immediately. The date and place that he should add had been given to him by the higher-ups. Someone must have spotted some drone prototype in that region. He played the clip once again. Of course it was incredible—who would be filming a stupid forest at dusk?

8

Terrence checked his personal email one last time before going to bed. There were the usual spams, but one message caught his attention. It was addressed "To Terrence Kovacs." All spams usually began with "Dear Sir," "Beloved in Christ" or some other idiot's name. He had never posted his real name on the internet. He didn't even sign his emails to his few friends (Frank and Louie) or family—which consisted of his mother only. His first thought was someone had hacked into his personal professional account, but that would be a huge security breach and very, very unlikely.

He opened the message, expecting to find the usual bull-shit and the link you had to click on to get a nasty virus.

"Dear Terrence, I urgently need to talk to you. Give me a date and place. I am in New Petersburg. T.T."

Terrence reread the message a couple of times. Thomas Thomassen. *WTF?* So many questions crowded his mind that he decided to call Frank and Louie and go out drinking.

Maybe they would have some ideas. Maybe they wouldn't. But it would be great to see them anyway. And get drunk.

9

"Wow, that *is* weird," Frank said, wiping the beer foam off his mustache.

"Did you have the email address traced and checked?" Louie asked, always the practical one.

Frank and Louie both worked for Counter-Intel, but in other sections. Frank was officially linked with "Logistics," and Louie with "Communications," but everybody knew this could mean anything. Terrence's own department was "Strategic Planning."

Frank was a little older than Terrence, dressed in civilian clothes, like him. His hair was curly and blondish, with patches of gray, especially in his goatee. He wore small rectangular thick tinted glasses which made him look like a mad professor of some kind, especially since he was dressed like one too.

Louie always wore his uniform, which was impeccably ironed. Terrence wondered if Louie ironed his clothes himself or if his wife did it for him. He had a beautiful childish face, with deep set blue eyes and dark hair. Terrence remembered seeing him at the academy and thinking *This is what Michael could have looked like if he had lived.* They had become friends almost instantly. Coincidence? Coincidence, no matter how you looked at it.

"Yes, of course, I had it checked. But nothing. I mean, it got lost in proxies. You know the deal. Probably temporarily 'borrowed' anyway."

"Man, that would freak me out if someone contacted me in my private mailbox," Frank said. "I thought the Army had guaranteed us total security."

"I filed a complaint," Terrence said.

Louie slowly rolled his half-empty pint glass between his hands.

"Unless the Army did it," he whispered in a half-voice, although the bar was almost empty.

"How do you mean?" Terrence asked.

"Yeah, how do you mean?" Frank echoed.

"I mean it could be some kind of internal security test, from a rival department. Remember that the Navy and the Air Force are also competing for credits. It's a tough game. Maybe Terry is being set up in a leak-test or something. I don't know; it's just an idea. Probably a dumb idea . . ."

Terrence shook his head. Yeah, it would make sense. The untraceable guy, the untraceable email, the new Dark Shield theory.

"To paranoia," Terrence said, lifting his glass.

"Hell yeah," Frank said, raising his glass too with a large grin. "To paranoia, indeed!"

IO

The empty apartment, late at night. Terrence was drunk. He sat down on the sofa and turned on the TV. Who were Frank and Louie? He meant, *really*? They had known each other for more than ten years but then again, what did that mean? He tried to find an answer in the blinding and blinking images, but to no avail. The images only cared about reflecting themselves on the surface of his eyes.

II

"UFOs spotted over the Eiffel Tower for the first time!"

"Giant UFO follows commercial airliner for twenty minutes"

"UFO sighting over the plains of Siberia!"

"Meteorite shower or UFO crash?"

Ah, the routine of work.

12

Closing Bergman's door behind him, Terrence was more confused than before. He had finally decided to tell the colonel about Thomassen's email, thinking it would be a wise thing to do, if Louie was right and it was just a security test. This would mean that Terrence was a reliable officer, who communicated with his superiors when confronted with possible security breaches. He expected Bergman to tell him to contact the Internal Security Department and not to worry; everything would be taken care of. The email would be traced and the sender identified.

But things had taken a strange turn.

"Is that the same guy you met in New Belleville?" the colonel had asked.

Terrence had nodded.

"Try to meet him, then, and see what he wants."

"Excuse me, sir, but wouldn't this compromise my cover? I met him as John Tammen and this is my private email . . ."

"Don't worry about it. We will interfere if necessary. But you should definitely meet him. Consider this an order, lieutenant."

Bergman had never named his rank before. And that just added to the general weirdness of the situation.

13

"Dear T.T., okay to meet you. Where and when?"

Sending the message he felt like a traitor. A traitor to himself, his job and all of his beliefs. The worst kind of traitor.

14

The empty apartment felt good. Safe. He was in control here. The framed pictures on the walls were like familiar faces—stills of 1960s underground film classics.

For some reason, his mind veered towards Renée as he entered his tiny kitchen. Two good years together. Until she had insisted on seeing his place, but Terrence wouldn't have that. Couldn't. This was his castle, his fortress, his last refuge.

He had been able to avoid the problem for a while by lying. First, he was moving (for three months); then he was redoing the place (for six months); then there was a bad flooding which had ruined the bathroom and the bedroom (three months, with the insurance problems, etc.). Then it had become more and more difficult to find a lie: visiting family, helping out a friend who was divorcing and staying with him . . .

Renée had finally had enough and told him that she believed he was actually married and didn't want to tell her. He had nothing to oppose her that could convince her.

He still missed her and sometimes, when he smelled someone wearing her perfume, his heart made a strange noise inside, like an ice cube cracking as it lands in the whiskey in a glass. But he had no choice other than to let her go. And his sex-life had been a collection of shallow but nonetheless liberating one-night stands for three years now. He poured himself a glass of whiskey to take the edge of the day off and was ready to toast with Renée's sexy ghost when the phone rang.

15

"I'm fine, Mother . . . I'm fine, thanks. And you?"

(. . .)

"Oh, work is fine . . . Yes. I'm still happy there . . . Good colleagues, yes. And it's always interesting. Well, most of the time, at least . . . Ah ah ah! What?"

(. . .)

"What?"

(. . .)

"No, no girlfriend yet, Mother. Sorry . . . Ah ah ah! Don't worry, I'm sure I will find somebody . . . It's just a question of finding the time . . ."

(. . .)

"Yes, I'm very busy. But I like it like that . . ."

(. . .)

"I know, Mother, I know. And how are you? How is New Babylon treating you? And how is Albert? Still playing bridge? . . ."

After the phone call Terrence took a long hot shower. It was always so stressing to talk to Mom. It felt like his loneliness was suddenly exposed and had become an enemy.

16

The New Petersburg museum of modern art was a brand new and almost blinding building set on a cliff overlooking the growling blue ocean. It was entirely covered with aluminum tiles and built in a shape reminding him of 1950s flying saucers. It was actually nicknamed "The UFO." *Perfect place for a meeting*, Terrence thought as he crossed the parking lot towards the entrance.

Could it been considered a coincidence? No, probably not. Thomassen had made this choice deliberately. If not coincidence, then irony. Or hint. Or symbol. Terrence shook his head and hurried on. *A man thinking too much, that's what I am. A man thinking too much.*

17

Terrence recognized Thomassen immediately, although he had changed his hair color and had grown a half-assed beard. As agreed, he was sitting at a table in the museum's cafeteria, reading today's paper. Terrence carried the same paper, a classic in espionage films.

A young woman was sitting at the table too, and Terrence stopped in his tracks. That wasn't part of the deal. He scanned the area to look for undercover agents, but couldn't spot one. Either the guys had become incredibly good, or there were none.

But the woman did make it seem like some trap had been set. And if she was the bait, she was the most beautiful bait he had ever seen.

18

Her hair was blonde and half-long, her face an oval with sharp features. She was dressed in a short jean jacket, a white top and blue jeans. Completely simple and completely '70ish. She also had incredibly beautiful black eyes, reminding Terrence of those Aztec obsidian knives they used in human sacrifices. Archeologists said that the victims were willing. He understood why now as he walked towards the table, his mind full of white noise and interferences.

19

Terrence sat down at the small round table. He had ordered a *latte* at the counter, which he carefully put down before him. Thomas put away his newspaper and the girl stared at Terrence defensively.

"How did you get my mail?" Terrence asked immediately.

Thomas looked away.

"We have our ways. We know a lot more than you can imagine."

"And who is this?" Terrence asked, indicating the young woman.

"My name is Vita," she said, looking straight at him without smiling.

Terrence felt something burn on his face. It was his cheeks. *Fuck, this is ridiculous*, he thought. *Pathetic.*

"OK, why did you contact me? What do you want from me?" he resumed, trying not to look at her instead of Thomas—and failing.

"We have been following your tracks for a while. We know you are working for the New Petersburg Counter-Intel Department and that you have many aliases. One of them is John Tammen. That's the one I met in New Belleville."

Terrence said nothing, trying to hide this surprise. *Could Louie be right? Could this be a setup from another defense department? Or was that bastard Bergman testing him?*

"I see," he answered, noncommittally. "Who are you?"

Thomassen and the woman who presented herself as Vita looked at each other.

"It is too long to explain here. We mean no harm. On the contrary, we have contacted you to warn you."

"Me?"

"No, not just you. The Earth."

20

You remember when you thought you had hallucinations? Of course, you were too young to call them that. You were only eleven, after all. You thought you had been dreaming. But you knew you hadn't. And you thought you were going insane. You remember that very well, don't you? "Crazy" was the word you used in your head, not "insane." But it meant the same.

21

"The Earth?"

Thomas or whatever his real name was moved uneasily on his chair.

"Listen, we can't speak here. I just wanted to meet you so you knew we were serious. But we need to meet again somewhere else. I'll contact you."

Terrence was about to protest when a loud crashing noise made him turn his head. A woman had dropped her tray, breaking the plates and glasses in an explosion of glass and cheap porcelain. The clerk from the counter ran out of his booth to help her with a pile of paper napkins.

"I don't know what happened," the woman apologized. "I suddenly went blank . . ."

When Terrence turned back to talk to Thomas and Vita, they had disappeared.

22

The following days, Terrence kept his eyes peeled, trying to notice anything unusual. For some reason, Thomas and Vita had made a strong impression on him—and not just because of the girl's beauty.

They were definitely scared, and probably crazy too. And they did know a lot about him. Terrence had chosen not to tell Bergman how much they knew during his debriefing with the colonel. It was better to play it safe, in case Bergman was part of this scheme.

The question that was really nagging Terrence was if—*if* he was being tested, why him? What had he done wrong? Or was this just "usual procedure," a routine exercise imposed on all agents?

Sitting in his little office, he kept staring at his screen without being able to form a coherent thought. He was working for a system, protecting it from people that either distrusted it or plainly wanted to destroy it. The system was supposed to be grateful, not suspicious of him.

Then again, he tried to reassure himself, *the system might not be involved*. But this thought was even more distressing, and he only wished he would never hear from Thomas and Vita again.

23

The two girls look like hippies, one with a denim mini-skirt, the other with a suede one. Both are wearing white t-shirts. The man is already lying on the bed, bare-chested, barefoot and in white jeans. The girls begin kissing the man each in their turn. He caresses the one in the suede miniskirt while the other girl undresses. That one is a blonde, the other a brunette. They are soon all naked and doing their thing. When they have finished, they lay next to each other, the man in the center, and they laugh.

24

Was the apartment lonelier because of the erotic films, or was it the same, with only an echo of possibilities? Was reality changing while he was watching vintage erotica on his laptop? Were the elements of his life gathering or falling apart around him when pleasure overwhelmed him?

25

Nothing seemed to have changed at work; the office remained the same, the conversations with the colleagues revealed nothing out of the ordinary. Little by little, he began to forget about Thomas and Vita, locking them up in a soundproof dungeon at the center of his mind.

26

Some people said that reality was just a computer simulation. The chance that it was true was 1 in 2. In a way, Terrence found it very reassuring.

27

"I want you to build up something around the Northern Sierra sightings. Code Four. You know what to do."

Bergman pushed a USB key across his desk. Various aliases were already flashing in Terrence's head.

"What's on the key?" he asked.

"Some footage you have to use. Usual procedure."

Terrence nodded. Code Four meant serious tampering with the material.

"Offensive or defensive?"

"Defensive."

"No problem."

"Any news from that Thomassen and his girlfriend?"

The question took Terrence by surprise.

"No, sir. Nothing."

"You would tell me, wouldn't you?"

Bergman's eyes were looking straight at him. Ice nails.

"Of course, sir."

"Good."

The colonel smiled. Terrence smiled back. Mirror effect.

28

Five luminous globes flying in formation over a highway at dusk. In the background, the Northern Sierra, looking like grayish blue drapes frozen solid. Obviously filmed with a phone from a moving car. No soundtrack—might have been erased by the Intel people. They did that sometimes.

Terrence knew what to do. The five orbs became three. He added a soundtrack from another video. He inserted randomly generated images between some frames: some with numbers, others with jumbled words.

When he was finished, he uploaded it on his most cryptic site, and forwarded the result to Bergman. That would send the UFO conspiracy theorists on a wild alien goose chase for a while. And this was what it was all about, actually: the control of time and space.

29

When Terrence was finished, he realized that it was late in the evening and that he was hungry. His office felt tinier and barer than ever. Maybe he should buy a plant to create volume and an illusion of comfort? He stood up and stretched. A picture of himself buying a sandwich from a street vendor flashed behind his eyes. Bright neon lights. The smell of the warm concrete. People brushing past you. An illusion of belonging.

30

The three strippers were dancing to the sound of '60s music. He had never tried this club before. Their bodies moved in a whirl of psychedelic motives. He loved it. Taking a sip of his expensive cocktail, he leaned forward and slipped a bill in the leopard panties of one of the girls. She smiled at him and wriggled lusciously. Her hair was blonde and bobbed up. Maybe a wig. Fake eyelashes too. Everything artificial. Wonderfully artificial.

31

As he walked out of the club and down the red-light district's main street, Terrence wondered what Vita would have looked like in the late '60s. It was just a thought, but he lingered on it like an oversweet piece of candy, rolling it over and over with his tongue inside his mouth until he found a cab and went home.

32

He crashed directly onto his bed, diving into sleep like it was a dark and welcoming swimming pool.

33

Like in all good espionage films, Terrence's phone rang in the middle of the night. He sat up in his bed, trying to weed out his dreams from reality. His hand mechanically grabbed the phone on the night table. Its clock said 3:45.

"Allô?" an unknown voice said.

"Allô?" he answered, still confused.

"Mr. Kovacs, sorry to ring so late. It's urgent. We have to meet now."

The voice sounded far away and strangely deformed.

"What? Sorry, but who are you?"

"We need to meet now! It's extremely urgent!"

Even deformed and panicked, the voice sounded vaguely familiar.

"Thomas?"

"Behind the Kino Palace Cinema, in the parking lot."

"But . . ."

Thomas—if it was indeed him—hung up. Terrence stared at the darkness, the phone still in his hand.

34

Life is full of secrets. That's no news to you, right? And you started early. You were eleven. You were old enough to understand that some things couldn't be told. And yet, you told little Michael, your best friend. You told him and he believed you. You told him and he died two days later. And even if nobody can control the weather, it was your fault. She had warned you, and you didn't listen.

35

Terrence scanned the deserted parking lot, but saw no one. His breath was short and his back was sweaty under his t-shirt and light jacket. It was at walking distance from his flat, and he had hurried to get there. Maybe he had arrived first. No cars were parked, and there were no shadow spots to hide in, thanks to the bright post lights illuminating the empty space. He decided to wait and see.

When Terrence looked at his watch again, he had been standing there for fifteen minutes. He decided to give Thomas another fifteen, just for the hell of it. He thought this could be a good setting for a murder scene in a movie, or a long artsy waiting scene. He could be the main character. People would feel sorry for him. It would be a very long and moving fifteen minutes.

3

virus database outdated

I

As soon as Terrence arrived at work, he went down to the cafeteria to get a large coffee to go. He hadn't slept much and he needed some fuel to make it through the day's routine. The Styrofoam cup weighed nicely in his hand. It felt like it contained all the reality he needed. Burning and black.

2

The probability of getting a royal flush as a first hand in poker is 0.0032%. Of course, you would say the cards were badly shuffled or that your opponent is a cheater because nobody, ever, would believe in such luck.

∃

"The Hollow Earth Theory beyond Nazi Occultism."
"Is your boss a Reptilian?"
"Whatever happened to the Synarchy?"
"My girlfriend was abducted by Aliens and I was arrested by the cops."

4

Locking his office, he thought again about Thomas and Vita. What the hell was this all about? What was going on? Was *anything* going on, actually? The emptiness of the situation suddenly struck him. It was as if a foreign hollowness had occupied his own hollowness. The elevator doors opened and he stepped inside. In the mirror, he noticed he still had his security badge around his neck. His picture looked at him. He avoided his own eyes.

5

Was his life a book or a movie? Certainly not a play. In a play, there would be many other actors. Unless it was a monologue. Was his life a monologue? He had never looked at it under that angle. *Maybe, yes*, he said to himself.

6

He ate a quick dinner made of leftovers and watched TV for a while. There was a new Scandinavian crime series that everybody at work talked about. He thought the story was good, but hated the photography. He found it artsy and pretentious. Like his own life. He smiled at his own joke, although he wasn't sure he had meant it as a joke.

7

The doorbell rang, waking Terrence up from a dreamless sleep. He opened his eyes, staring blankly at the dark ceiling. *What the hell?* The doorbell rang again. Actually, he hadn't realized it was his doorbell at first. He hadn't heard it in so long, except for the occasional plumber or janitor visit. He realized now how much he hated that stupid two notes melody.

8

It was her. Although her face and shape were deformed by the spyhole (what a perfect name!), he recognized her immediately. Vita. He saw her lift her hand to press the buzzer again and he opened the door.

She pushed him inside without saying a word and slammed the door behind her. Her breath was short and she was wearing the same clothes as the first and last time he saw her—a jean jacket over a white tee and a pair of jeans. Incredible he could still remember that. She also had a duffle bag which she dropped at her feet.

"What the . . . ?" he said, still caught between a very strange dream and a very strange reality.

"Shhh!" she said and lifted her index to her mouth.

She gently pushed him inside the apartment, and suddenly he realized how amazingly alone he had been all these years.

9

"Can I have a glass of water?" Vita asked him before he could say anything.

He took a glass in the kitchen and filled it with tap-water. His brain was beginning to function more clearly, but the more he felt awake, the crazier the situation seemed.

She gulped the glass down, wiped her mouth with the back of her hand and collapsed on the couch. He grabbed a chair and sat down next to her. She didn't look at him, just stared at the empty glass rolling between her two palms.

"Tom is dead," she finally said. "They killed him."

"Wait . . . What? Who killed him? When?"

Thoughts like crossed electric wires. Smell of something burning inside. The fat around the heart?

"A few hours ago. They will say it was an accident, but they killed him. They always say it's an accident. I saw it, but they didn't see me. I need more water, I'm always dehydrating too fast."

Terrence picked up the glass from her hands and went into the kitchen to refill it. The cold drops sprinkled on his fingers made him feel better.

"Thank you," she said accepting the glass.

"Where did Thomas get killed?"

"At the corner of 7th avenue and 18th street. We were coming out of an Indian restaurant. I had to go to the bathroom, so he went out first. I was coming back when I saw him being pushed in front of a car. I saw it through the glass door. It went very fast. Tom didn't have a chance. They will say that he was drunk and fell in front of the car, but that's not the truth. He was pushed. I saw it."

"Who pushed him?"

"Someone. I don't know. I just saw a shadow. It was dark outside."

"Did you contact the police?"

She looked at him for the first time.

"Are you crazy? The police are involved too. The top brass, at least."

Crazy? Who was crazy? Not him. Her? HER? He shrugged. A mental ping-pong match was going on in his head. *Crazy? Not crazy? Who was crazy?*

"Hmm, so what is your plan now? Why did you come here? Isn't it dangerous? For you? For both of us?"

She shook her head. Her hair, her eyes, so beautiful.

"I wasn't followed. I made sure. They don't even know I exist, I think. I'm not on their radar yet. Tom didn't know I existed until I contacted him. That's why he came to New Petersburg."

Terrence thought for a second.

"How did you find Tom? I looked all over the Net for info

about him, and I found nothing. Nothing."

"That's because his name was not Tom, and he had a site under another name. It was coded, that's how I found him."

The answer was so simple it made Terrence blush with shame. *Professional agent, right?* If all this was a test, he was failing in a big way.

"What's the name of the site?"

"It doesn't exist anymore. He took it down before coming here."

"I can still find it. I have ways."

"Why do you want to find it?"

She was looking straight at him and the blackness of her pupils fascinated him.

"To verify your story."

"You don't believe me?"

Terrence smiled like a psychoanalyst in a TV program.

"Of course, I do. Still . . ."

Vita shrugged.

"Whatever. The site's name was 3 Lyr."

She spelled it out to him.

"You won't find it."

"We'll see."

Vita looked around the room, as if she just suddenly realized where she was.

"Is it OK if I stay with you for a few days?"

"Yes, sure. Of course."

Terrence felt that his desire had spoken before his mind. Because he wanted to kiss her right here, right now, his hand in her beautiful hair, his chest pressing against her breasts.

What is going on with me? Am I going insane?

"Of course. You can take the couch tonight. We'll switch

tomorrow, when I have put some clean sheets on my bed."

Insane. Yes. Completely, utterly insane.

IO

The chance for a cat to land on its legs is 1 in 1, depending on the height of the fall. The last part is the most important element, and it tends to be overlooked. The height of the fall.

II

The first thing Terrence had done after sitting down at his office desk was to check Vita's info about Thomas's supposed death. Someone had indeed been killed where she had said the night before—he found a small article on the local online paper. The victim had allegedly been drunk and had jumped or fallen or slipped in front of a speeding van. His identity was not revealed.

They will say that he was drunk.

Terrence kept staring at his computer screen. Tiredness and confusion danced a devil's waltz behind his eyes, preventing him from concentrating.

They will say that he was drunk.

Typical line from an espionage movie, no? Vita could have witnessed the accident and interpreted it as a murder, if she was delusional.

But was she? The obvious answer was: yes. *As they would say.* But he wanted to make sure. He picked up his phone.

"Louie, it's Terrence . . . Fine, thanks . . . Listen, can you check something for me? It's a site, that has been deleted. Name: 3 Lyr. Three, L-Y-R . . . Could you check it out for me, see if you can find it? Eventually link it up? Yes, it's work, not a personal thing . . . Thanks, buddy! Let's grab a beer soon . . ."

Not a personal thing, as they would say.

12

Were you delusional during that summer night, when you were eleven? Yes, they would say. You knew they would say that. That's why Michael was the only one you told and he was killed. And then you knew you hadn't been delusional. That it had been true and scary. So scary you still didn't want to think about it today.

13

Vita was still sleeping on his couch when Terrence had left to go to work earlier in the morning. He wondered if she would still be there when he came back. He didn't know if it was a wish or a fear. Or both, in an uncanny new combination.

14

It was late in the afternoon when Louie called him back. Terrence was actually about to leave his office, eager to rush home and check if his unexpected guest was still there. But he saw Louie's name appear on his phone and accepted the call.

"Took me all day, but I found it, buried deep in one of the web's trash cans. Pretty strange stuff, actually. I saved the page and linked it up to your email. You can check it out yourself."

Terrence thanked him, feeling his heart beat faster. So the page did exist, after all.

"By the way," Louie resumed, "I know it's none of my business, but next time we have a drink, maybe you can tell me more about this page. I'm very curious."

"Sure. No problem," Terrence half-lied.

He sat down at his desk again and turned on his computer. Two things that Vita had said proved to be true. The first question was: how true? The second was: what truth was that?

15

The page consisted of a poorly arranged blog template, without any frills. Just the title, written in Times New Roman font, size 36, "3 Lyr," and a long series of numbers separated by semicolons and blank squares indicating that the symbols could not be read by the program. *Well,* he thought, *the site did exist. But what the fuck was it about?*

He downloaded the page and forwarded it to the Cryptographic Dept, where he sometimes sent text and images to have them checked for secret messages. *The plot thickens,* he thought again.

That was: if there was a plot.

16

In the subway, on his way home, he watched a young man with a baseball cap playing some game on his telephone. His thumbs were moving at incredible speed. Terrence had never any inclination to play computer games, although he was, by his own admission, a complete nerd. But he found games boring, because they were pointless.

You never changed level in real life; you never gained any power-ups, whatever the incredible scores you attained on the machine. You just remained the same, with actually less and less qualities and powers. That kid, in fifty years, will not have achieved level 215 and unlocked special bonuses: he would have severe pain in his thumbs from arthritis and his cap would hide his bald and wrinkled scalp.

17

The TV was on when Terrence unlocked the door of his flat, meaning Vita was still here. She was watching the news, a mug of coffee in her hand. His mug. He glanced in the kitchen, and saw the remnants of a meal. She had made herself at home.

"Hi," he said. "I'm back."

"Did you find the site?" she simply asked.

This girl wasn't ready for small talk.

18

Terrence had ordered Chinese takeaway and was digging his fork in his Colonel Ming noodles, or whatever they were called. He wasn't good with Chinese names and chopsticks. Vita was eating her fried rice with vegetables. It was the first time in a long, long while that he'd had a guest for dinner. It felt strangely good.

"So . . ." Terrence finally asked, "How did you get my private phone number? How did you find my address?"

"That was easy," Vita said with a smile. "You've just got to know how to look and where to dig for info."

Terrence shook his head.

"My info is confidential. It's very well hidden—for obvious reasons. Honestly, I have to tell you I think you might be working for a foreign secret service, although I don't see why you would contact me. I know nothing interesting. I only work with the UFO-sphere, as you well know. So, why me? What is this all about?"

Terrence heard himself thinking out loud. He didn't like the way his voice sounded: professional, paranoid.

"I don't work for any foreign secret service. Not in that sense, anyway. We've contacted you because we need your help. Well, now, I need your help."

"My help for what? Why was Thomas murdered?"

Vita sighed and pushed her plate away.

"It's very complicated. While I was looking for someone to contact, Thomas was doing the same. I finally found Tom, and he had found you. Synchronicity at its best."

She smiled and Terrence smiled back. *Was she wearing a wire? Was all this being taped?* If he was being tested, all this conversation could be used against him.

"Sorry to interrupt," he said curtly. "Are we being record-ed? Are you wearing a wire? Are you testing me or trying to frame me?"

"What? No! No!"

She suddenly lifted her t-shirt, revealing a classic black bra and a beautiful chest.

"Happy?"

Terrence felt his ears burn.

"Sorry. I just had to ask."

Vita shrugged, her face frozen in an ironic pout.

"And what about you? Are you wearing a wire?"

"Me? Of course not!"

He laughed nervously.

"Show me. Come on, show me!"

Shaking his head, Terrence reluctantly unbuttoned his shirt.

"Good," Vita said. "Can we trust each other now?"

He nodded. Point made.

"So, why me?" he asked again. "What for?"

"It's a long story, but I will make it short. I am from a planet in the Lyra system. You haven't detected it yet, so let's call it Planet X. You can't pronounce its name in your language. I am here to liberate the Earth."

Terrence opened his mouth, then closed it slowly. Had he been hit by a car and was in a coma? Had his food been spiked at the cafeteria? His mind reared like a wild colt.

"Excuse me, can you say that again?"

"I am from Planet X, in the Lyra system. I am here to liberate the Earth, and I need you to help me."

19

The most frightening part in that gibberish wasn't actually what Vita had said. It was the uncanny feeling of *déjà vu* that had suddenly possessed Terrence.

You are eleven again. You are still a child. You never grew up and now you're still alone with your secret. Your crazy secret, you crazy fuck. You crazy, crazy, CRAZY fuck.

20

There is a 6.8% chance of a nuclear war starting between major nations within the next twenty years, killing more people than World War II.

21

Terrence had poured himself a large glass of whiskey on the rocks. Vita was now sitting on the couch, and he had decided to join her. This bad craziness abolished distances.

"Okay," he said. "If I get you right, you are an alien who is trying to protect us from other aliens?"

Vita nodded, her beautiful eyes shining darkly under the lamp hanging over the coffee table.

"And it was an alien who killed Thomas?"

She shrugged.

"No, it was a human. Many are working for the Empire."

"The Empire?"

"I can't tell you everything right now. I'm still not sure I can trust you."

"I understand," Terrence said, thinking: *of course you can't.*

She suddenly grabbed his free hand. It felt warm and human.

"Thank you," she whispered.

Her face came close to his. Her lips parted to welcome his tongue.

"This is a good way to begin trusting each other," she said while he kissed her smile.

22

At the cafeteria, he smiled at the woman attending the cash register. For the first time ever. She didn't smile back.

23

Flesh-colored fragments glittered in his mind as he tried to concentrate on his work. The Lyra system appeared in 14 novels, 8 films, 2 comics and 8 computer games. Anybody could claim they came from there. Anybody. More wonderful erotic images troubled his vision.

24

Terrence had scanned the news for more info about Thomas's death, but nothing came up. He decided to call the city's hospitals, pretending to be a relative looking for his brother. It took him five calls to finally get an answer at the Saint-Sebastian clinic: yes, they had received the body of a John Doe that night. He had been hit by a van while crossing the street. Somebody had picked it up, though.

"Family?"

"I can't tell you. It's not written down. That's funny. It should be. But there's no signature. Just the official document stating the removal of the body. They must have forgotten to ask. We often hire people at the morgue who have no qualifications, I must admit . . . It's hard to find people to work here . . . Well, you understand."

25

A murder, no body, the Lyra system. Bad craziness. The logical thing would have been to confront Bergman directly and ask him if he was being tested.

The logical consequence would be that Bergman would send him directly to the shrink, and he would possibly lose his job.

Logic seemed to be the problem here. Maybe even the problem all-around.

26

Frank had called to ask him if he wanted to meet later in the evening at their watering hole, with Louie. Terrence had accepted, feeling he needed a break.

"Do you want to come?" he asked Vita later, at the apartment.

She was sitting on the couch, reading something on her tablet. She shook her head.

"No, I want to lay low for a little while. I want to be sure I'm off their radar. Did you notice anything unusual today, by the way?"

Terrence shrugged. "No, nothing."

She smiled as he sat next to her.

"Listen," he said. "I checked the hospitals to find Tom's body. It was at the Saint Sebastian Clinic, but someone picked up the body. Did Tom have any family here?"

"No, I told you. He came from Viborg City to meet me."

"Did you pick up his body?"

Vita laughed.

"Me? This is crazy? Why would I do that?"

Crazy? Who's crazy?

"To frame me? To make me believe things?"

Her two hands suddenly framed his face. Warm towels at the Chinese restaurant. Wonderful feeling. Her eyes dug into his.

"No, I didn't pick up his body to make you believe me. Once you know the whole story, you'll know I'm telling the truth."

"So tell me. You told me you wanted me to help you."

Her hands left his cheeks. They still tingled.

"Soon. I will tell you soon. I promise. Go out with your friends, have a good time and tomorrow, I will tell you. Everything."

Terrence nodded and reached in his pants' pocket.

"Oh, by the way, I got you a key to the apartment from the janitor. You can leave this apartment and come back whenever you want. You're free."

She took the key and gave him a little kiss on the lips. He kissed her back, intensely.

Crazy? Who's crazy? Me, me, ME!

27

Louie and Frank were in a good mood, and the place was packed. They exchanged the usual jokes and covered the usual topics, the trodden territories of friendship. They also discussed some politics, which was their friendly all-out boxing ring.

"And what about that page I sent you? Anything new?" Louie suddenly asked as Frank ordered a new round.

"What page?" Frank asked.

"A web page I found during my research on some topic," Terrence answered, hoping Frank would get the "none of your business" innuendo.

"Really weird stuff," Louie resumed, to Terrence's dismay. "Just a title and some numbers. Crazy weird. Oh, and it had been deleted too. Took me ages to find it."

"Would love to see it," Frank said. "Is it part of your test, you think?"

Terrence shrugged.

"Maybe. No idea. Well, yeah, it could. Probably. But I can't show it to you. It's classified material now."

"Shucks," Frank said.

Sometimes a lie is a truth, Terrence thought. *It's just a question of perspective.*

"Was it some Eastern Confederation code page? Like, co-ordinates for their nuclear submarines or something?" Louie joked.

Terrence shrugged, taking a mysterious air. The conversation veered back to trivial matters, like women, death and the universe.

28

Vita was sleeping in his bed, when he came home. He contemplated joining her, then decided to sleep on the sofa. He didn't know if the last time they did their thing had been a spur of the moment kind-of-situation, or if she really liked him. *Better safe than sorry*, he thought, shutting the bedroom door behind him and stepping into his sitting room.

As he undressed clumsily—he couldn't remember how many beers he had drunk—he suddenly noticed Vita's tablet on the sofa.

He sat down on the couch and picked it up. Hesitatingly, he turned it on. It was locked, of course, with a four letters or numbers code. Absentmindedly, he typed "Lyra," then "Vita" but nothing happened. As a last try, he typed "PlaX" and it worked.

He stopped breathing a few seconds and listened. Nothing moved in his bedroom, so he examined the tablet. There were the usual game and photo apps. He looked at her picture gallery. Nothing but a few selfies in various places. Five, to be exact. One was in his apartment. There also was a documents file—but it was password protected and neither "Vita," "Lyra" nor "PlaX" worked.

He gave up, not wanting to push his luck. The last thing he checked was her browser, but she had erased all its history. Her tablet was as blank and mysterious as she was. After all, there was a balance in the universe.

29

He dreamt he was back in his childhood house, in the suburbs of New Petersburg. It was a hot summer night and he couldn't sleep. The window of his bedroom was open and a faint breeze moved the curtains. The electronic alarm clock indicated 1:35. Luckily it was the holidays; he wouldn't have to get up early to go to school.

A peal of thunder suddenly rocked the house, followed by a blinding white light which illuminated the entire room. He jumped to the window, but saw nothing. He was disappointed: a thunderstorm would have made the temperature drop. *What a strange dream*, Terrence thought within his dream.

30

It's not a strange dream, you stupid. It's a memory. You are eleven and this is not a dream. You are and will always be eleven. Always.

31

Someone was shaking him gently. Terrence opened his eyes. Vita was next to him.

"You were whining and moaning in your sleep. I came to see if you were alright . . ."

Terrence sat up. *I am not eleven years old.*

"Yes, yes. Must have drunk too much . . ."

Vita caressed his hair. Electricity ran from his scalp to his hips.

"We can share your bed, if you want. It's more comfortable."

They kissed. Her mouth was warm and welcoming. He suddenly thought of an old episode of Star Trek, in which Captain Kirk was seduced by a beautiful alien woman. Kirk's heart was broken in the end.

32

They lay in the empty darkness of the bedroom, Vita's head resting on his chest. He caressed her soft blonde hair, thinking of Monica Vitti.

"I have to ask you this again: why me? Is it some sort of test? Have my superiors sent you to seduce me to see if I'm a 'weak link'? I don't care if that's the case. I would do it all over again."

Vita lifted her head and he felt her chin dig in his ribs.

"Planet X sent me. Nobody else. And we chose you because of the information we gathered from the Net. From your profile, you seemed the most likely to help us."

Terrence sighed. He didn't want to say it, but he felt he had to.

"You know it all sounds completely crazy. Nobody would believe me if I should tell them. They would probably lock me up, and you too."

But I'm not crazy. I'm not crazy.

33

Then you saw her, standing alone at the end of your garden.
The girl. She was slightly shining, dressed in a strange skirt,
her hair cut in a page. She was dressed like someone from a
long time ago. Your grandparents' time maybe. She saw you
and lifted a hand, a gesture you only saw Indians in Westerns
do when they meant "Peace." Without really knowing what
you were doing, you lifted your hand too. She didn't open her
mouth, but you heard her voice.

"Come," she said.

You shook your head, because you were afraid. But she
repeated "Come!" in your head, and her voice was friendly, so
you carefully went down the stairs and into the garden. You
were half afraid, half wishing your parents would wake up.

The little girl took your hand. It was warm and tickled
lightly, as if she was surrounded by static electricity. You followed her into the small woods behind your house and you saw
her spaceship. Because that was what it was. A spaceship—a

large silvery object floating in a halo of light.

The little girl smiled and brought a finger to her lips.

"You can't tell. OK? You can never tell!" she said in his mind.

You nodded. Tell who? Everybody would think you were crazy. They would lock you up somewhere. Forever.

"If you tell . . ."

She frowned and made a threatening gesture with her hand. Then she smiled again.

"I have to go now, but I will come back. For you. I promise."

She gave you a small electric kiss on the cheek and disappeared in the light. It flew straight up into the sky and disappeared.

You walked home and climbed back in bed. You could still her gentle voice saying "I will come back for you" until it faded in some weird electric noise, but you knew no one would believe you and hoped—really hoped—it was only a dream. Then dawn came and you realized you hadn't slept at all.

34

"Okay, I will tell you the truth now," Vita said, sitting up next to him.

He could smell her in the darkness, a haunting sweet and salty smell.

"Like I told you, I come from Planet X. We were colonized a long, long time ago. But some of us decided to resist. Unfortunately, it was too late for Planet X. But there is still some hope for Earth. That's why I was—or we were—sent here."

"Colonized, by whom?"

"They don't have any name that we know of. We call them 'The Subliminal Empire.' They don't have any materiality, not in our sense anyway. And they feed on control."

"Invisible aliens?"

"Immaterial, rather. And Earth is their next target."

Terrence tried to put aside the last remnants of his rationality for the time being. Vita's voice and body were too tangible to contradict.

"Why Earth?"

"Earth is a transition zone, a hub if you will. It is a place where many worlds meet. One of your writers, Burroughs, he saw it. He wrote about it. About the Subliminal Empire too, although he called it "The Nova Mob." But it was the same thing."

Terrence had read some Burroughs when he was a student and hadn't understood much.

"A sort of an 'Interzone,' then?" he said tentatively, trying to impress her with some Burroughsian terminology he could remember.

"Exactly. That's why it's so important for the Empire. It opens up to other worlds and dimensions."

"But how does the Empire gain control? I mean, if you're here, that probably means they're here too, right? Tom was killed by them, right?"

Vita kissed him softly on the forehead and rubbed the spot as if she wanted it to go beneath his skin.

"Yes, he was. And the Empire has been here for a long time. How long, it is impossible to know, because they keep changing History."

Terrence caressed her neck and shoulders.

"How do you mean?"

"If you read the news, the events change constantly. You think they're the same, but they're not. The Empire modifies your perception of History constantly. They do the same with science. If you read archeological and scientific pages, you will see that. Archeologists and scientists keep coming up with new theories all the time."

Terrence couldn't help smiling in the dark.

"It's because science progresses. Our knowledge becomes better. That's why. We just know things better."

"So can you predict the weather accurately for the next ten days?"

His mind drifted to the Weather Channel and their continuous mistakes.

"Good point. But still . . ."

"Who is the ancestor of man? Who were the first inhabitants of America? Did Hitler die in the Bunker?"

Terrence shook his head.

"I'm sure that one day . . ."

"And what about food?"

He looked at her, perplexed.

"Food?"

"Why do you think people enjoy an industrially-designed hamburger and French fries? Is pop soda really so fantastic? Or raw fish? Or vegetarian dishes? And why do people love shit music?"

"Wait! I don't get it? You mean the Empire is controlling everything we think we like? "

Vita shook her head.

"No, not everything. I can see they're not powerful enough yet. But it's growing."

"But if they're immaterial, how do you know they're here?"

"By the accelerated presence of media and the exponential development of self-metaphorization of your societies. That's one of the symptoms. They infect language. Meaning disappears and becomes replaced by something else, which resembles a meaning, but isn't one."

Terrence felt a crack in his rational shell. This did sound

familiar. This sounded like his job. He opened his mouth, and closed it again. He had nothing to say to this. Vita lifted her head and pressed her lips against his.

"Do you believe me now?" she whispered.

"I believe you exist," he answered, feeling himself growing hard against her warm belly.

"It's a start," she admitted with a smile.

35

Vita was still sleeping when he left for work. He felt like he was too, although he was awake. Well, he thought he was awake. It was what made the most sense, if any. He climbed in the subway car. Everybody else seemed to be sleeping, though.

4

classified

I

Bergman's door was open, and he stood up behind his desk to greet Terrence.

"You wanted to see me, sir?"

"Yes, close the door, please."

Terrence obeyed and sat on the chair facing the colonel. He tried not to show his nervousness, but it was the first time he had been called by Bergman without any explanation. Did they know about Vita? Had Louie leaked his query to his higher-ups?

"I know we haven't had much interaction," Bergman began, opening a file on his desk, "but I felt you deserved to know what I thought of your work."

"Yes, sir."

The test, Terrence thought. *It's all about the test. He's going to fire me.*

Bergman quickly scanned the typed report in front of him, then looked up again and smiled.

"You're doing a great job, Kovacs. A truly, terrific job. I keep getting compliments from the top, and it's mostly thanks to you. I wanted you to know that."

Terrence felt his cheeks burn, like a little kid in a Japanese anime.

"Thank you, sir. I really appreciate this."

"That's why I recommended you for a promotion. And it arrived today."

Bergman handed him a sheet of paper.

"Congratulations, Captain Kovacs."

Terrence shook the extended hand in disbelief.

"Thank you, sir. Thank you very much!"

"It's OK, Kovacs. Now get back to your office and keep doing that great job of yours."

2

The chance of finding a shiny Pokemon is 1 in 8192. The chance of finding your perfect partner is 1 in 285,000. You've got to love that Pokemon.

Terrence hadn't watched any '60s porn since he had met Vita. He wasn't surprised, but he wasn't relieved either. He sort of missed it, like one misses cigarettes. Vita hadn't smiled or laughed after they had done their thing. Not once.

4

In the subway, he thought about the Subliminal Empire as he looked at the ads running along the cart walls. A conspiracy within a conspiracy. Only someone completely paranoid would think of that. William Burroughs had that reputation too. "Language is a virus" he had written. He suddenly realized he hadn't asked Vita her last name. There were still things he yet had to discover about her. So many things.

5

Vita had cooked some spaghetti with vegetables. It smelled terrific, and Terrence felt his stomach rumble. She had also bought a bottle of Italian wine and set the table.

"Honey, I'm home!" he joked, catching her by the waist and kissing her.

He suddenly felt he was playing a scene in a 1960s American comedy. Was this staged? Was he, too, being manipulated by this Empire?

"What's wrong?" Vita asked.

Terrence touched his forehead.

"Nothing. Just a strange feeling, that's all."

"Like you were acting in a movie or something?"

He stared at her.

"Yes, exactly. How do you know?"

"I sensed it. It's a Planet X thing. We keep some of our powers when we incarnate."

"Incarnate? Powers? Wait a minute, I need some wine."

Another weird feeling of déjà vu creeped into his mind as he poured himself a glass. *A scene from a film? What film?*

Vita leaned against the sink.

"To come here, I had to incarnate—become a human. That's who I am now. And sensing is one of my powers. Sensing and provoking, they're the two powers I have left."

"Provoking?"

"Making things happen. Like when the woman tripped in the cafeteria when we first met. Remember?"

Terrence nodded and took a sip. The wine was excellent. "You did that?"

Vita nodded. Another thing impossible to prove or disprove, apart that it *happened*.

"So you can read my thoughts too?"

Terrence heard the anguish in his question. Vita shook her head.

"No, not really. But I can sense things, and put images to them. That's how I know how you feel right now. It's typical for subjects trying to free themselves from the Subliminal Empire's grip. The mental associations become obvious, superficial, annoying. I'm glad you're feeling that, actually. It's a good sign. Shall we eat? I hope you'll like it."

The food was excellent too. Maybe cooking was also one of Vita's superpowers? He smiled at his own joke, but didn't tell her. He wasn't sure people from Planet X had a sense of humor.

6

"How can you free yourself from the Empire?" he asked her as they lay in bed. Her shoulder against his felt like a comforting soft rock. She ran a finger against his cheek. He felt like making love again. He wondered if she could read his thoughts at the moment.

"There is a way. A drug. It can free you."

"A drug?"

"Yes. It's called Synth. You might have heard of it . . ."

Of course he had heard of it: it was on the news all the time. A new synthetic drug, that caused ravages. People were going crazy, killing other people or offing themselves in spectacular suicides.

"That's what they tell you," she said. "But it's not the truth. It's a counter-drug, in fact. Like apomorphine. It cures the addiction. We created it on Planet X. It makes you see things as they really are. How beautiful reality is. Non-compromised reality, that is."

"Are you a Synth addict?" Terrence asked, again, worried.

That would explain everything. Everything. He felt both devastated and comforted. Vita shook her head.

"No, I don't need it. I see both the world as it is and as it should be. But I am here to help the Earth. I have a Plan B and you're going to help me. You promised, remember?"

He actually didn't remember promising anything, but he said yes, he would, anyway. She kissed him and took control of him through his desire and that was perfectly fine.

7

She had said she had a plan, but wouldn't tell him about it yet. Terrence typed in some key words in the search engine. A plan she had yet but wouldn't tell him about. One of the key words was "Synth." Yet she wouldn't tell him plan about. He waited the necessary nanoseconds. Tell him wouldn't yet about the plan. "Synth: designer drug. Unregistered in database. Composition unknown." Him she wouldn't yet plan tell him about. He sighed. He had to contact some people.

8

For the first time in a long while, Terrence decided to look out of the large cafeteria windows. The sky was blue, with a few fluffy clouds sailing slowly over the army base's roofs. Wasn't this real? What were his eyes not seeing? Was he an I, a him or someone else? Was he a character in a book written by himself or by someone else? Was the sky empty or full of invisible bacteria-like aliens? Was he going insane or was he already insane?

9

"I told you I saw her! She was real!"

"A little girl? In your garden? At night? And she left in a spaceship? You were dreaming, Terry!"

You and Mike are in his room, sitting at the foot of his bed. You just came back from playing ball in the backyard. You're both sweaty and flushed. You have been thinking all afternoon about telling your friend about the little girl. He's your best friend, you were sure he would understand. You're almost regretting having done it now.

"I swear to God I wasn't dreaming! It was real! She told me she would come back for me!"

"Why? What does she want with you? You're not even that good in sports . . ."

"I don't know. I never asked her."

"You stupid or what? I would've asked her."

You absentmindedly played with one of Mike's large toys lying on the carpet. It was a Star Wars cruiser ship.

"I'll ask her when she comes back," you said.

"Cool," Mike said.

You also remembered you had promised not to tell. Two days later, little Michael was struck by lightning on the school playgrounds. You never said a word about that night and had since decided it had all been a bad dream. Although you had always wondered, deep down inside, if the little girl would come back for you one day.

10

Terrence dialed Todd Bailer's number on his cell phone. He was standing in the parking lot behind the cafeteria because he didn't want anybody hearing his conversation.

Bailer was an ex-academic who had claimed to have visited the Realm of the Dead and who now hosted the NPTV show "Incredible truths & Other Hidden Mysteries." Terrence had met him a couple of times under his Serge Tarpofsky alias, impersonating an Alien conspiracy theorist who debunked all alien conspiracy theories, except those he deemed "credible."

They had become friends, as they were, in fact, both skeptics and had continued to email or call each other over the years. Todd had invited him on his show four times, giving Terrence's alias a large media coverage which had benefited his undercover work.

"Hey Todd, it's me, Serge."

"Hey! How are things?"

"Fine, fine! You?"

"Business as usual. Swamped in the weird."

They both laughed shortly.

"I have a question for you, if that's okay . . ."

"Sure! Shoot!"

"What do you know about Synth? I mean the drug, Synth?"

There was a pause, and Terrence could picture Todd thinking.

"Well, honestly, I don't know. People use it, and the media are going ballistic over it, like when LSD was around in the '60s and '70s, but I couldn't really find anything about it. Sure, some people's brains got fried, but just two or three. Not the figures you read or hear about."

"Do you know where it comes from? I heard some people say it's an alien drug."

Todd laughed heartily.

"Yeah, I heard that too. Crazy, right? I think it's a hoax. But to be honest, some things are strange about this drug. Are you alone? Can I speak freely?"

Terrence scanned the parking lot. The closest person was a woman at the other end getting into her car.

"The coast is clear."

"About a year ago, I wanted to do a show on Synth and that alien connection. Permission was denied. I asked my producer, 'what the fuck,' right? He said there were orders from above. They said it was because they feared it would be publicity for the drug."

"Makes sense, no?"

"Well, you know my show. It's mostly a debunking show. I was going to do that. But no, it's strictly forbidden to talk about it. Sounds like political censorship to me."

"Did you file an official protest?"

"You kidding? I want to keep my job. I don't give a damn about drugs anyway. Had my share, if you know what I mean . . ."

Bailer had claimed one could visit the Realm of the Dead by ingesting a specific drug that some shaman could brew. This provoked great hilarity in the scientific world and caused Bailer to resign from his academic position. It also made him a New Age guru and a famous TV host.

Terrence thanked him and promised to meet for a coffee soon. "They said it was because . . ."

They said. They said.

II

What chapter was his life now? Still number four or had he hopped to number seven or eight? More important: how many chapters did his life have?

12

Back in the office, Terrence decided to check Synth one last time. He logged in to the government list of illegal drugs. There was a long series of names, all with hyperlinks. He found Synth and clicked on the link. "Information classified." He scanned the Net and visited a few conspiracy sites.

A chemist pretended to have the proof that Synth was actually a genetically designed alien drug. There was a long blurb with a lot of scientific details and diagrams.

Terrence chose an alias and sent him an email. It bounced with a Mailer-Daemon message. Unknown or disconnected address. He did a search with the guy's name. He had been a chemistry prof at some New Petersburg high school, but had committed a drug-related suicide about a year and a half ago.

Terrence massaged his face. Was this bad craziness or just plain craziness?

He also checked his professional email. The Cryptology Department had run a "negative" on the 3 Lyr page. Couldn't make sense of it. Classified it as "Unexploitable," which meant "Crazy mumbo-jumbo" in their language.

Figured.

13

At the apartment, he found Vita talking on the phone. She was wearing a short summer dress and looked stunning. She blew him a kiss as he put down the champagne bottle on the sofa table. He had bought it at the corner store to celebrate his promotion. He wondered who she could be talking to. She had never mentioned friends or contacts.

"Champagne?" she asked as she shut her phone. "Wow! What are we celebrating?"

"A good day at work. Who were you talking to? Not that it's any of my business, of course . . ."

She shrugged.

"A friend of Tom's. He's part of plan B."

"Of course."

Terrence nodded, but felt a knot in his stomach. He was afraid that if all this was a dream, reality would be even worse when he woke up.

14

They were sitting on the sofa, Vita's legs across his own. They felt weightless. He was caressing her thigh, enjoying the silk of her bare skin. The bottle of champagne stood half-emptied on the coffee table.

"What is this Plan B you're talking about?"

She smiled.

"I'll let you know when it's ready. Actually, I've got to go now," she said, swinging her legs away and standing up.

She gave him a little kiss on the lips and was gone before he could get up. Only her perfume remained, like a light summer rain quickly evaporating under the sun. He realized he couldn't place it.

15

Was he still being tested? If so, why did he get his promotion? It didn't make any sense. As if anything made any sense right now. A woman from Planet X. A murder that looked like an accident and a body that could not be traced. The Subliminal Empire. Mind Control. Terrence sighed and poured more champagne into his glass. If he was going crazy, he should at least do it with class.

16

Terrence was already sleeping when Vita joined him under the sheets. He had waited for her late into the evening, finishing off the bottle and watching a stupid action comedy on TV.

She snuggled against him and her naked warmth spread along his spine. He turned around and kissed her. She smiled. A clip from a '60s erotica film jumped in his mind and he smiled too as she wrapped her thigh around him.

17

"Are you mind-controlling me?" he asked after they had done their thing, their bodies still sweaty and throbbing. "Or are you dick-controlling me? Is that also one of your powers?"

Vita's hand softly brushed his cheek and chin.

"No," she answered.

And he didn't believe her.

18

During his coffee break at work, Terrence decided to go up to the terrace. He did that sometimes when he needed to think more clearly. The vastness of New Petersburg extending flatly in all directions was like a concrete mantra to him.

There were a lot of clouds in the sky, but enough patches of blue to keep hopes up. He looked at the infinite blue canvas, trying to get a glimpse of the invisible. Of course, he failed, but that was actually reassuring. In more ways than one.

19

"10 incredible UFO conspiracies that might actually be true."
"Europe's largest UFO secret bases."
"Former NASA employee reveals what is really behind the UFO conspiracies."
"20 facts about the 13,000 years old Black Shield UFO."

20

"How was work?"

Vita was sitting on the couch, looking at some documents on her tablet. She hadn't turned the lights on, sitting in the half-darkness, her face slightly glowing from the tablet's screen.

"Fine."

He went into the kitchen to get a glass of water, turning on the lights of the apartment in passing. He hated not being able to see clearly.

"And what you're looking at?" he asked, sitting next to her.

"Plan B."

"Can I see it?"

She shook her head and shut her tablet.

"Not now. Later, when everything is arranged."

"You're not going to kill people, are you?"

Vita laughed. She sounded genuinely amused.

"No! Of course not! We are pacifists, not like the Empire. We believe in freedom, not death, or control, which is the same thing."

"Death and control?"'

Bad craziness, he thought again. *But she is so goddamn beautiful.* Vita put her tablet aside and grabbed his hands.

"I know what you're thinking," she said playfully. "You're asking yourself again if I'm crazy. Well, I'm not. Not at all. I am from a planet in the Lyra system and I know how the Empire works. As long as the control is maintained, they don't need to do anything. And if they're threatened, they can use people to help them."

"Like with Tom?"

"Exactly."

Terrence thought for a second. He now craved something strong, like a good glass of whiskey.

"Do these people helping them know they're controlled?"

"No, but they enjoy being controlled. It gives them the illusion of power, like a pop singer, a religious figure or a president can have."

She might have a point, he mentally conceded. *Then any anarchist has, also.*

"Okay, so what is that reality I, or we, humans don't see?"

"You want to see it?"

"Can I?"

"Yes, it's very easy."

Terrence's mind flashed a "Warning" sign. More awkward TV references.

"How do you mean, 'easy'?"

"That easy."

Vita took out a small cellophane package. It contained

about four of five flat white pills.

"What is that?" Terrence asked, alarmed.

"The drug you call Synth."

"This is highly illegal . . ."

"I know. I told you why. You want to see the world as it is, or not?"

Terrence's drug life floated behind his eyes. It was a very short film.

But she is so beautiful. So beautiful.

"OK, then. OK. Are you going to try too?"

Vita shook her head.

"I don't need it anymore. I used it before. I see the world as it is. All the time."

She smiled and handed him a pill.

21

How long had they been walking? Did it matter? He had never seen—nor felt—the city so beautiful. The evening sky, the buildings, the lights, everything seemed to shine and vibrate. The clothes of the passers-by glimmered too, as if made of silk or other precious cloths.

Vita passed her arm under his. It was the first time they walked together outside. The air was full of an extraordinary perfume that blended with Vita's but was ten thousand times more powerful. The cars passing by were all vintage models, some makes unknown to him, but nonetheless beautiful.

In the beginning, the music coming out of the cars' stereos sounded horrible, a mishmash of commercials and repetitive notes and voices, but he managed to tune into other fabulous melodies. It felt like he was listening to the soundtrack of his own life, and it was amazing. He had never seen his life as a Cinemascope feature. Vita looked absolutely stunning, her skin changing nuances at they strolled in the near empty street.

The only dark spots in this colorful mosaic were the billboards, or the radiophonic commercials. The billboards were all empty and gray, the commercials pure static. He had never felt so, so . . . free?

Yes, you fucker. Free. Exactly. FREE.

Are you okay? she asked him.

Yes, absolutely, he answered.

He smiled as he realized they hadn't used words.

22

"How are you feeling?" Vita asked him as he woke up next to her the following morning.

The alarm had just set off, and she had stopped it. A shy sun shone through the rolled-down curtain. Terrence blinked a couple of times then smiled.

"I feel . . . great. I really do."

He felt changed too. Deeply changed. He now felt what Tim Leary must have felt the first time he had taken LSD. But was it the same? Just a terrific acid trip?

"The Synth will still be active for a few hours. Enjoy it while it lasts."

Vita got out of bed.

"Your coffee will never taste so good, I promise . . ."

23

Terrence took a break between his usual blogging and scanning-the-web activities to check out more pages on Synth. The only material he found was the usual bullshit, either claiming it was the wonder drug that could cure all ailments (a statement to which he wasn't far from subscribing at the present moment, he had to admit) or that it was the most dangerous mind-altering drug ever (which could equally be true).

He wondered if he knew anybody in the department who would have access to more info.

He sent an email to some guys he was in contact with in the Research & Development Unit, with Bergman in c.c. It was better to get the boss somewhat in the loop, so his query wouldn't arouse unnecessary suspicions.

Yes, this time don't fuck up. Remember little Mike. Remember the chances of being struck by lightning.

24

Vita was waiting for him with some Chinese takeaway. She had chosen his favorite dish, and favorite beer.

"Am I so easy to read?" he asked.

"Yes," she said, opening his bottle of Tsingtao beer for him.

25

Going to the bathroom, Terrence noticed a large plastic bag from some department store on his bedroom floor.

"Did you go shopping today?" he asked when he came back.

Vita turned on the TV and nodded.

"Kind of. It's Plan B."

"Really? What is it?"

Vita got up. She had chosen a sports channel. Synchronized swimming. Even after the effects of Synth had disappeared, it looked strange.

She walked back into the room and sat down, the bag on her lap. Terrence peeked into it. There was a white powder in another locked plastic bag.

"What is it? Plaster? Flour?"

"No. Synth. Took me all afternoon to crush those goddamn pills . . ."

Vita laughed and Terrence felt his heart stop.

"Wait . . . Wait . . . How much Synth is there in this bag?"

"About 700 grams. It should be enough."

Thoughts collided in Terrence's mind in terrifying train accidents.

"Enough for what?"

"For Plan B."

"What is Plan B?"

He had almost screamed. *This was more than bad craziness. This was prison. For life, maybe. This was serious. This was no-more-fucking-around serious.*

"Relax. Everything is under control. I mean it. We're going to free this city first, and if we are successful, we will know we can free the Earth . . ."

"Listen, I can't . . . I really can't . . ."

He took a deep breath.

"I love you. I really, really do. From the first time I saw you. But I can't help you commit a crime . . . I work for the government, you know that and . . ."

Vita took his hands in hers. Her black pupils reflected tiny versions of him. Her hands were soft, her eyes were deep.

Are you mind-controlling me? Are you dick-controlling me?

"I just need you to drive me somewhere. It's absolutely safe. I don't even have to tell you what I'm going to do. You're perfectly innocent. More than you even think. You drive me and I come back later. And nobody will know it's me, and nobody will know it's you. I swear. I know these things. I can feel these things."

She sounded so convincing.

Are you mind-controlling me?

"Give me some time to think, OK? Just a day or two. I

can't decide now. I can't. I'm afraid of losing you, and I'm afraid of going to jail."

She smiled.

"Neither will happen. Do you want one?"

The pill was tiny in the flat of her hand. He picked it up and swallowed it.

Are you dick-controlling me?

26

"Allô?"

(. . .)

"Mother?"

(. . .)

"Yes, yes. Everything is fine. Absolutely fine."

Vita, looking like a goddess standing at the corner of the street.

"I'm just taking a walk. I might go see a film."

(. . .)

"I don't know. I'll decide when I get there."

(. . .)

"No, not alone. With a friend."

(. . .)

"You don't know her."

(. . .)

"Yes, it's a 'she.' But she's just a friend, Mother. OK? And how are things with you?"

Synth moved inside him like a delicious chocolate milk-shake. Vita walked to him and gently nibbled his earlobe, making him shiver and laugh.

"What? Nothing . . . Just the wind. It can be cold this time of year."

He pushed Vita back, laughing silently.

"Glad to hear you're well. Listen, I've got to get to the theater . . ."

(. . .)

"Yes, love you too."

He hung up and put away the phone in his jacket pocket. Vita took his arm and they hurried towards the cinema. But to him, they were hurrying towards freedom in a whirl of lights and sounds.

27

"You wanted to see me, sir?"

"Yes, Kovacs. Sit down."

Terrence did as told. The Synth had worn off earlier in the morning. Bergman looked his boring old self.

"This is . . . delicate. And I want you to know that I am only an instrument here . . ."

"Yes, sir."

"I have received a call this morning, from high above . . . It was about your Synth query, remember?"

Terrence nodded. Of course he did. It was only yesterday.

"Well, I don't know it's about, but they don't like it, up there." He pointed an index to the ceiling.

"They told me to tell you, you should stop whatever project you're working on with that drug immediately."

"Sir?"

"I know, I know. I'm sure you're doing this for the best interest of our city, but it seems that you're either stepping on some sensitive feet, or the matter is taboo. They mentioned 'national security.' You know what that means, right?"

"A threat?"

Bergman moved uneasily on his chair.

"Not from me, of course. But I would do as I tell you. I would focus on some other UFO-Alien conspiracy theme if I were you. I would, like, drop everything about Synth right now, clear my browser if I need to do that, erase all my documents on the subject . . . Do you get my drift?"

It was the first time Bergman had actually looked concerned about something. Terrence felt strangely moved. And frightened.

"Yes, sir. I will do as you advise me. Immediately. Consider the case closed."

"Thank you, Kovacs. I was sure you would understand."

Bergman winked at him and shook his hand. Terrence thought about the 700 grams of Synth powder sitting in his apartment and winked back.

28

The water reservoir was located in the outer limits of the city, at the top of the surrounding hills. From here, one had a beautiful view of the city: it looked like a plowed dark field sown with thousands of light seeds, moving in different directions at an invisible wind's whim.

The night breeze blew through the rolled-down window, gently caressing Terrence's face. He had parked the car about a kilometer away, in a dark spot. It was a deserted area, and one could see other cars coming from a distance. He looked at his watch. 1:45 a.m. Vita must be in by now. Maybe even finished. It had been more than half an hour. She had told him she would give him the signal when she was finished.

He had asked her a lot of technical questions about her Plan B—how she would get in, how she would avoid surveillance cameras, find the reservoirs, *etc.*—but she had just told him not to worry, she had her powers, there would be no problem and they would wake up to a new, free world. He had understood she was protecting him, giving him as little info as possible. "I just need a driver," she had said. "And a driver doesn't need to know anything."

Synth was enhancing his vision, making him see every detail of the cracked road, the little stones, the fallen leaves. An amazing photography of reality. He had never felt so a part of it, except when the little girl had taken him to her ship. Emotion tightened his throat. She had trusted him. He had failed her. Mike had died. He wouldn't fail Vita. He wouldn't fail himself.

He looked at his watch again. Time was passing slowly. He hoped Vita would call him soon. Or send him an SMS. Whatever the "signal" was. He wanted her back, next to him. Forever.

29

Dawn found him asleep behind the wheel. Vita hadn't come back. Panicked, Terrence looked at his phone. Nothing. No message, no SMS. Had she been caught? Was she being interrogated? He started the car and drove slowly along the plant. Nothing seemed out of the ordinary.

There were two guards in their little gatehouse, chatting. No police cars, no strange military activity. Nothing. He U-turned further down the road, and drove past again. One of the guards saw him and glanced at him before resuming his conversation with his colleague.

Terrence wished Synth had given him special telepathic powers, but it definitely hadn't. He decided to drive back to the apartment, call in sick for work, and wait for Vita to show up. Because she was going to come back, he kept telling himself as a desperate mantra. She was going to come back.

30

Did the water have a strange taste? He tried it again, uncertain. Maybe. Maybe not. It was difficult to tell. He looked out of his kitchen's window. The street looked normal, with its low buildings and shiny TV antennas. He turned on the radio. The usual commercial crap began to fill the space. Although . . . Terrence pricked up his ear. It sounded distorted, maybe?

Or was it just the reception that was bad?

Vita still hadn't shown up. He walked back into the sitting room and turned to the news channel on the TV. Nothing about a failed terror action against the city's water reservoirs.

He almost wished they had caught her. At least, he would know where she was and what had happened. He went into the bedroom and went through her duffle bag again. Had he missed anything? Only her clothes were piled in. He took out one of her t-shirts and smelled it. It was clean, but he imagined her perfume. He was sure she would come back.

Like the little alien girl? She would come back and bring you to her planet in her silver spaceship, with a Neil Young song in the background?

Yes, why not? He had tried Synth and had felt the real, free world. He had felt it and he longed for it.

"She will come back!" he said out loud.

Then he felt a little ridiculous, walked back into the kitchen and tasted the water again.

31

Terrence sat down at his office and turned the computer on. He had been on sick leave for three days. Officially, he'd had a bout of influenza. He had bought some Kleenex to make it more believable, and blew his nose when talking with colleagues.

Was the test over? Was it why she had disappeared? Or had the Empire caught her?

He logged in his John Tammen page. He had a new piece on the Black Shield to write, to dismiss other theories.

Subvert and protect.

Protect who?

Vita's face materialized in front of him. She could at least have left him some Synth.

32

"Drugs and the alien influences on musicians."
   "DMT, Aliens and reality."
   "Can psychedelic drugs help us speak to aliens?"
   "Do aliens do drugs?"

About the Author

Seb Doubinsky is a bilingual writer born in Paris in 1963. His novels, all set in a dystopian universe revolving around competing city-states, have been published in the UK and in the USA, and translated into numerous languages. He currently lives with his family in Aarhus, Denmark, where he teaches at the university.